Unfinished Business

Brie Kraus

To any who have been accused of something, but were innocent.

Unfinished Business

Chapter 1

Tears rolled down her eyes that morning. The water inside the droplet of the tear was so peaceful that it was soon rubbed off by the woman who released that tear. Tammy Williams stood in the bathroom one morning. It was a normal morning, as nothing else had changed since that day. Everything was back to normal. Tammy had been back at work for six weeks, and nothing out of the ordinary had happened. As usual, she had gone back to investigating gang killings in the area. She was bored. She was sick of her job, and sick of life. It was fair to say that she had been feeling depressed since she was told the news that her boyfriend had suddenly died; she did love him, after all. Although nobody was to blame for the death other than Danny, Tammy could not help but feel angry, wanting justice for Danny, even though there was no justice to be served.

Tammy returned to the office, where everybody else sat.

"Are you alright?" asked Miranda, who Tammy detested.

"I'm fine," Tammy lied. She just wanted to heave herself through the day and wait until the next day.

She had tried to speak to her mother about it, but it was no use. Even her aunt, who was a vicar, could not help. It would only take time for Tammy to get over his sudden death, although how long that would take was debatable.

As usual, Tammy was assigned her next task, to discover who had murdered a member of the top gang member in town. It made her sick, how people could just go and kill others for no reason. Today, Tammy and the team were doing some desk research, into the key suspects and witnesses.

During the day, they conversed, as usual, and then one topic came up that Tammy wished not want to hear about.

"So," said Pam Hobsworth, "I saw Barry Scott yesterday."

Even the mention of that name made Tammy sick. Barry Scott was a serial killer, and he just happened to be the only person who Tammy did not manage to bring justice to. She hated him, and the thought that he was still out there, living his life, while the relatives of his victims were devastated, their lives turned upside down, all because of him.

"Really?" said Miranda. "Where was he?"

Miranda knew that Tammy hated talking, or even hearing, about Barry Scott, but she continued to speak about him. She did not care for Tammy much, perhaps because she was jealous of her amazing sleuthing abilities.

"He was in the nearby shopping centre," replied Pam, "looking as happy as Larry, as always. He just makes me want to kill him!"

"I'm sure he'll get his comeuppance one day," said Graham Mitchell.

"He won't," Tammy replied, "he's too clever to be caught."

"People know who he is," Pam said to her, reassuringly.

"But not enough people. This case had to be thrown out, even though he pretty much confessed to me that he was the killer, and that's what gets to me!" cried Tammy.

Nothing else was said on that topic. Instead, they talked about the job that they were currently working on, in order to try and distract Tammy.

"Anyway, does anyone fancy going out for a drink tonight?" said Pam.

The others agreed to go, before Tammy did. Perhaps a drink was one easy way to forget about her troubles, she thought.

Chapter 2

They arrived at the bar, immediately after work. They needed a drink, all of them, because the week that they had was more stressful and tiring than usual; nothing had ever changed, and they all bored of the same routine. Tammy just wanted something dramatic to happen, like it did in Paris. Although that was a rather morbid thought, she wanted something to challenge her brain, for she feared that the lack of exercise was slowly killing it, eating away at it so that she would not be able to use it like she used to be able to. Times were changing, and Tammy had to accept that. Things were never as simple as they used to be.

As soon as Tammy entered the bar, she received the shock of her life when she noticed Barry Scott stood there! Time stood still at that moment, for Tammy's eyes widened. She just could not believe her luck. He was there, with friends, laughing and joking, and there was nothing Tammy could do about it. Barry then noticed Tammy, and said to her, "Oh, hello, Tammy! How are you today!"

He winked at her; it sickened her. She just wanted to turn round and vomit on the floor, but she knew that she had to face up to him sooner or later, to try and show that he had not defeated her, even though he had. She hated him for that. Tammy turned her head and saw another group of people. They stared at her, making snide remarks. Tammy wondered why they would do something like that; she had never seen them before, or at least she thought she hadn't. She had come across many people in the job, so she did not know whether she had seen them before or not.

The group got the drinks in, and sat down, in view of Barry.

"We can't let him get to us!" cried Miranda.

"How is that possible?" Tammy asked her, trying to resist the temptation to look in Barry's direction, to see if he was looking.

"Well, we just show him that we are happy. That might make him upset."

Tammy gave in to temptation. She turned around, and, just as she thought, Barry stood there, looking at her, as if he waiting for her to turn round, knowing that she would. He winked at her for a second time, making her even more enraged.

"So, anything interesting happen to anyone lately?" said Pam, trying to start the conversation.

Tammy turned her head slightly, but not in Barry's direction. Instead, she looked at a woman in red clothing, sipping on a glass of red wine. She eyed Barry, and it was clear that she was flirting with him, even though she did not speak a word to him. Tammy just felt like getting up and screaming, "Don't do it! Your life is at risk!" but she didn't. She knew that she could not accuse Barry Scott of murder because there was no official evidence that it was him, even though she knew for a fact that it he had done it.

Then, Tammy remembered the last thing that Barry had said to her: "Do you like to hunt?"

She started to have sinister thoughts. Perhaps he was planning on killing her next? She knew that she could not think about it, because she just wanted to get out of there.

She felt a sudden urge to go to the toilet. She looked for the bathroom, and unfortunately, the door was right next to Barry Scott.

"Can you look after my keys?" she said.

Knowing that there was no escaping it, she got up to walk to the toilets. She knew that she needed to think fast about how to approach Barry Scott. Perhaps she would ignore him, but she knew that he would talk to her, saying some sort of smug comment about how she failed to solve the murders.

She was right. As Tammy walked past Barry and into the toilet door, he said to her, "so, we still ready for that hunting trip?"

Tammy ignored him. She went into the bathroom, and when she came out two minutes later, Barry was still there, laughing and joking with a bunch of half-drunk men.

"Are you alright?" Pam said, as Tammy sat down again.

It took Tammy five seconds to answer that, but she lied when she replied.

"Yeah," she said, trying to put on a brave face.

Chapter 3

Tammy looked at the table where the five people were. She did not know them, but they knew her. She tried her best to listen in to their conversations, to see if she could work out who they were.

"I wish he was dead!" cried Linda Bell, a middle aged woman who was also there. She then turned round and glared at Barry, although he did not notice her, and not caring to.

"I can't believe he murders our relatives and gets away with it!" yelled an enraged Joseph Hart, the father of one of the victims.

Tracy Bradley, the mother of the youngest victim, just sat there, crying again.

"I'd do anything to bring justice to my boy," she said.

"Believe me, love, any one of us would," cried Bess Salting, the young daughter of one of the victims.

"And there's that bitch detective who failed to solve the case," cried William Salting, the brother of Bess, and ten years older than his sister.

Tammy knew that they talked about her, but she did not wish to make a scene. so she sipped her drink, continuing to listen.

"I agree with you there," said Linda. "She deserves to be sacked!"

Tracy Bradley had had enough.

"I'm going out for some air," she said.

"I'll join you," added Joseph Hart, jumping up to follow her.

Tammy thought that was rather strange. She began to think sinister thoughts; perhaps they were plotting to murder Barry Scott? It was a possibility, and it had happened before; and given the mental state that that group was in, it was certainly quite likely, although Tammy did not want to get involved anyway. If they were going to do it, she would let them get on with it.

Tammy turned round and saw Miranda talking to the woman in the red clothes. She looked like a tart, in Tammy's opinion, but since Miranda was chatting to her, she must have been a decent person, thought Tammy.

"Don't say anything," said the woman, whose name was Angela, "but I'm planning on getting with that man tonight!"

"Which one?" asked Miranda, dreading the inevitable answer.

Angela pointed to Barry Scott. Inside, Tammy felt like vomiting. Could Angela be his next victim?

"He's a dangerous man," Miranda tried to explain to her, but Angela did not listen. and stopped talking to Miranda, approaching Barry, who was still at the bar, and started dishing out flirtatious compliments towards him.

Five minutes later, Tammy had had enough. She walked out, unable to face that man any more. Unfortunately, on her way out, she caught Barry Scott kissing Angela round the side of the pub.

"Ah, hello!" said Barry.

Tammy was so sick of it. By now, four or five other people stood outside of the pub, smoking.

"You make me sick," said Tammy, in a slow tone of voice.

"Do I?" he said.

"You know that you won't be free forever! You'll be behind bars sooner or later!"

By now, Miranda and Pam had also left the building.

"Really?" said Barry, "and why do you think that is?"

"Because you're a serial killer!" cried Tammy, getting excited.

"We've been through this," Barry replied, "I did not kill anybody. You have no evidence of that, and you will never find any evidence of that. I'm sorry, but you've lost on this one!"

"So, you're confessing?" said Tammy, trying to force it out of him once and for all.

"No," said Barry, "just telling you the facts. You will never catch the killer if you keep going on at me. Let's face it, even if I was the killer, you would not have been able to catch me, so that makes you a really crap detective, doesn't it?"

Tammy felt so small inside.

"I'll tell you something," she said to him quietly, going right up to him. "I'll see you get what you deserve one day, even if it's the last thing I do!"

Barry laughed.

"I'll get you!" screamed Tammy, almost slapping him on the face, but Pam stopped her.

"Come on, get back inside," said Pam.

Tammy refused.

"I'll walk home!" she said.

Before she left, Tammy gave one last glare at Barry Scott. He smiled and winked at her.

"See you soon," he said.

"Do you think Tammy will be alright?" said Pam, back inside the pub.

"She'll be fine," said Graham, more interested in drinking his beer.

About twenty seconds later, a scream was heard. Everybody rushed outside, where they found Angela standing over the body of Barry Scott, in shock and unable to move.

In the dark background, Tammy emerged and watched what had happened. Barry Scott stood in exactly the same place as he was when he was last seen by Tammy. Everyone gathered round the body of Barry Scott, not knowing what to think. Tammy approached him, and looked deep into his bloodshot eyes. It was clear that Barry had suffered a terrible, painful death.

Chapter 4

The police returned to the station, surprisingly. Miranda was the first to speak.

"So, Tammy, what is the name of that perfume you always wear again?"

"Euphoria," Tammy replied, enjoying the fact that she did not care about the death of Barry Scott.

"Alright, you've made your point," said Pam, "but you know that we are going to have to investigate this murder?"

"Yes, I know," Tammy sighed.

"I hated that man! I don't understand why we have to investigate," Miranda said rather defensively.

"It's our job," Tammy replied in a pessimistic attitude.

"The first thing you can do is sort out the alibis of the five people on that table. They were relatives of Scott's victims, so they had a strong motive. We need to establish where everyone was then," Pam said.

"I'll get to it," said Tammy, knowing it was her duty. If she did not at least try to work out who the killer was, she would be in deep trouble, and she would not want to ruin her reputation as an amazing detective, even if half the town wanted Barry Scott dead, especially in that horrible, gruesome way.

Tammy tracked each of the five suspects on the same night, as they were still in the pub, excited about what had happened. They were celebrating, at least until Tammy came in.

"Oh, look!" cried Tracy, "here she is!"

"Here who is?" asked Tammy.

"Well, you murdered Barry Scott, didn't you?" asked Joseph.

"Why do you think that?" Tammy asked them, intrigued.

"Well, you were caught shouting at him, and not a moment later, he was killed! It does not take a genius to work out it was you!"

"Well, maybe you're not a genius," said Tammy, "and as much as I hated him, the five of you had stronger motives, didn't you?"

"But we have alibis!" said a drunken Bess.

"I'll have to talk to each of you individually," said Tammy, looking at the five of them and thinking it could have been one of them.

The first person who Tammy talked to was Tracy. As the mother of a murdered victim, Tammy did not think a prison sentence would make her suffer any more than she was suffering now. Tammy did not care if she was the killer, as Tracy had been through the worst thing that could ever happen to her in her life.

"So, Tracy, do you mind telling me where you were between the last time Barry Scott was seen alive, and when Angela found him dead?"

"Well," said Tracy, "to be precise, I was in the bathroom, with Bess Salting."

"Right," said Tammy, "I'll check up on that. Anyway, do you mind telling me about Barry Scott?"

"I'm glad he's dead, if that's what you're asking?" replied Tracy, "but I didn't kill him, because my son would not have wanted it to be resolved in that way. Barry Scott would have suffered in prison. That's where he should have gone—he'd have suffered more there!"

Tammy agreed with that, but since that could not be achieved, making him suffer a horrible, painful death would have been the next best thing. Tammy did not need to know much else, because this was a rather simple case.

She moved on to Bess Salting. She asked Bess where she was, and Bess said that she was in the bathroom with Tracy. Tammy needed to think about that later on. Next to be interviewed was William Salting, the brother of Bess. He said that he was at a table with Linda. Linda collaborated his statement, although there were no witnesses to this, and the CCTV evidence was waiting to be recovered. Finally, Joseph Hart said that he was outside, taking some air. Tammy was the most suspicious of him, although he was not definitely the killer yet. Evidence needed to be gathered.

"Why don't you just stop investigating this?" said Joseph. "He made a fool of you! Why don't you just accept that justice has been done and let the killer get away with it!"

"Because it's my job, unfortunately," said Tammy, "and I don't think a prison sentence would hurt any of you much more than you've already been hurt!"

Joseph left her.

Tammy returned home that night, and sat down with a nice glass of fresh orange juice; she had a big day ahead of her and wished to relax while she had the time.

Suddenly, she heard a piece of paper get shoved through the door. It's half past ten at night! she thought to herself. She opened the door to see who it was, but nobody was there; they had vanished. She picked up the piece of paper, and read the scratched writing:

Stop the investigation now or you will pay the consequences.

Chapter 5

The following morning was an early one. Tammy could barely sleep; she was too busy debating with herself about whether or not going ahead with the investigation was the right thing to do. Ignoring the threat that she had received the night before, Tammy thought about the morals of it all. On the one hand, she should go ahead with the investigation, because it solves the murder of somebody, and that is what she was paid do. On the other hand, she should not, because that would upset the relatives of his victims. It could have been argued that whomever killed Barry Scott had actually done society a service, by ridding the world of a serial killer. In the end, Tammy decided to continue the investigation to see how it progressed and where it would lead her.

That morning at the station, the others were still reeling with excitement about what had happened the night before. Barry Scott was dead! Tammy had to tell the truth to herself as it was like a massive weight had been lifted from her shoulders, because she knew that she would never give up fighting until he was behind bars, or at least, until justice was brought to him.

Tammy thought about something: the night before, when she received the threatening note, where did she put it? She had forgotten. As a matter of fact, she could not remember much about the night before. Was there a chance that she had dreamed it?

She walked in the room, and the rest of the team remained in silence. A knife could have cut through the atmosphere in there.

"What's the matter?" said a confused Tammy.

"We have nothing against you," said Pam, after a few awkward seconds of silence, "but we think that it is wrong, you doing the investigation."

"I went through this with you last night!" Tammy said.

"Just this once, let it be," Pam said, as if she were giving an order.

"I'm sorry, but I can't," said Tammy, "not yet, anyway."

"You look a little shaky," Miranda said, grinning slightly.

"I'm fine," Tammy replied.

Miranda decided to put pressure on her.

"You sure about that?" she asked.

"I'm fine!" repeated Tammy with more force. "Anyway, I'm more than fine! I am happy that Barry Scott is dead, if that is any consolation to any of you!"

Tammy took a seat.

"I remember the times he was acting really smug," said Graham Mitchell. "Well, we all had the last laugh, because he paid for what he did! I don't care which of the five of them did it, but I hope they don't get caught. They've lost their relatives, for crying out loud! Why would prison help them?"

"Alright, you've made your point!" exclaimed Tammy, feeling rather left out.

"What kind of upbringing do you think he had?" asked Pam.

"Probably sadistic," said Tammy, "judging from what I know about most serial killers."

"Libby...what's her name was not abused growing up. She was crazy!"

"Well, that's just one in a million," replied Tammy. "The vast majority of the time, serial killers have been abused, and there is a real reason as to why they kill people."

"Now it's that age old question," said Miranda, jumping in, "is evil created or are people born evil?"

"We'll never know," said Pam, finalizing the conversation.

The boss rushed in.

"Tammy, I need to speak to you!" he cried.

"Why?" asked a confused Tammy.

"Will you just come with me now," replied her boss in an irate tone.

Tammy followed him down the stairs in tense silence as everyone approached the car. Several police officers hung around the area, and even forensic scientists were there. What Tammy saw next shocked her completely: in the boot of her car, there was a crowbar, and on that crowbar was blood, and lots of it.

"What the hell!" she screamed. "How did that get there?"

"We are hoping you'll be able to answer that," said the boss.

"It wasn't me!"

"Look, this crowbar will be taken in for analysis, and it will be kept as evidence against you. I am not going to arrest you at this stage, but if any more evidence against you appears, I am going to have to arrest you for the murder of Barry Scott!"

Chapter 6

Tammy could not get over the shock. Was somebody trying to frame her? It certainly looked that way. If so, it was a race against time to catch the killer, or else, Tammy will go to prison for murder. She was scared now, because Mitchell thought it was her; she knew it, and was determined to prove him wrong. Nobody could prove that she did it, not yet, anyway. Was there more 'evidence' to come?

There was indeed more evidence to come. Unfortunately, later that day, more was when the police examined the perfume bottle that Tammy had used for the night before, suggesting that Tammy had been near Barry Scott, or in direct contact with him. His clothes had the same scent as Tammy's perfume, and several policemen confirmed that. This meant that Barry Scott had to have come in close contact with either the perfume itself, or someone who wore it for his clothes to possess the strong smell; and as no other explanation existed, it was assumed that Tammy was the one who had come into close contact with him. However, Tammy was not arrested yet as evidence was still circumstantial, although some of the police officers in the station did say themselves that they thought it was her.

Tammy was devastated. As a result of this revelation, had been sent home until further notice, because she was now considered a suspect. She cried all the way there, but nothing could be done.

"Do you believe me?" Tammy asked Pam.

"I'm sorry, I don't know what to believe," was Pam's last words to Tammy on the phone.

Tammy knew that she would resurface from this. She was more determined than ever to solve the crime, even though the most ironic thing was that it was the murder of the person she hated most, but she knew that she had to do it. She was losing support quickly, and therefore, knew that she needed to gain it again. Firstly, she had to think deeply about the killer, but there was not yet that much to go on, except for the "evidence" that was left to frame her. Somebody must have really had it in for her. She assumed that it was one of the five relatives of the victims, because they had the most motive.

Miranda came to visit.

"Come to see how I am?" Tammy asked in a fairly bitter way.

"Hello, Tammy," said Miranda. "I'm here to search your house to gather evidence."

"Why?" asked Tammy.

"You know it's procedure," Miranda replied.

"You know it's not me," Tammy protested.

"I don't know that," said Miranda. "I'm not assuming anything. That's what you always taught me in every case that we have done together. It could turn out to be the person you'd least suspect, and you have to keep that in the back of your mind."

"You know it's not me!" cried Tammy.

Miranda stopped talking and focused on her work. She put some latex gloves on. Tammy hated her more than ever now. After a while, she went into Tammy's back garden, and searched the flower pots.

"What's this then?" Miranda said, pulling out a knife from one of the flower pots.

"I don't know!" screamed Tammy, but Miranda took no notice.

"Tammy Williams," Miranda begun, "I am arresting you for the murder of Barry Scott. You don't have to say anything..."

At that moment, Tammy froze. This cannot be happening! Was her life about to end in tatters?

Tammy was put into the car, and one person even took a photograph. It still hadn't sunk in yet. Tammy knew that she needed to think of ways to prove her innocence, no matter how hard that would be.

Chapter 7

Tammy sat in a cell in the police station. So this was what it was like. She felt trapped. There was nothing there for her to do, except use the toilet and lie down on the thin mattress in the dark room. The window was very small; if there was a fire, she would not be able to escape the building, which would count as a health and safety issue, although it was ignored by all, because nobody cared about prisoners, guilty or not.

Eventually, a police officer came to give her some dinner.

"This is absolutely ridiculous!" she cried, but the police officer did not listen. "It wasn't me! Nobody can prove that it was!"

She knew that nobody would listen to her. After she finished her dinner, ten minutes later, the same officer came, and took her to the desk. She knew that was coming.

"Tammy Williams," said the officer at the desk, "you are charged with the murder of Barry Scott. You are refused bail."

"I'll prove my innocence!" exclaimed Tammy, "and I'll put a claim in for this mess!"

She was taken back to her cell. Tammy decided to make a start on proving her innocence by thinking about the evidence that was planted. Nobody could have gotten into her back garden without taking the risk of being seen. Tammy assumed that it was one of the five suspects who was doing this to her, if not all of them, but how could they have found out where she lived? She thought about the websites that helped one to track people, and assumed that that was how they had done it.

Knowing that the plant pot incident would get her nowhere, Tammy decided to think about the perfume. How did her perfume get on Barry Scott's clothes? She thought about that for a while. The final piece of evidence left to her was the crowbar found in the back car. Then, she remembered something: for five minutes, she had left to go to the toilet, leaving the keys on the table. Other than that, her keys were in her back pocket at all times, so nobody would be able to get hold of them. That five minutes would prove crucial to her, and she knew it.

She thought about where everybody was when she went to the toilet; the rest of the squad were there, and the five main suspects were also there on a nearby table, watching her every move like a hawk. That provided them with the opportunity to do it. Could it be possible that the five of them managed to distract the rest of the squad while taking Tammy's keys, before putting the bloody crowbar into the back of her car? However, there was one major argument against this: Scott was murdered after Tammy went to the bathroom, so it was impossible for a bloody crowbar to be placed in her car at that time. Was it actually Scott's blood on the crowbar? If not, then it would be dismissed as evidence. However, she refused put her hopes on it, because the murderer was an intelligent person, and Tammy knew it.

Seeing nowhere else to go, Tammy used her one phone call to contact a friend from the past…

Inspector George Coarse entered the building in a brisk walk despite having to use a walking stick; he had suffered an injury to his right leg the last time he had been seen there. He was allowed to visit Tammy for five minutes.

"Long time, no see," he said. "How've you been?"

"I really need your help," said Tammy, cutting to the chase because she knew that time was short.

"I know you need to get out of here, but how can I help?"

"I need you to find the real murderer of Barry Scott," Tammy replied.

"Aren't you supposed to be the one who can work these things out?"

"You're a great detective, too," she said, with a hint of desperation. "I've seen you in the papers a couple of times."

"I'll try my best, but I can't make any promises."

"You do this for me and you won't regret it," Tammy promised, seeing Coarse as her last chance.

Chapter 8

Coarse was not a complicated man, straightforward, who liked to get things done, and done right. He hated waiting. He wanted to stop Tammy from suffering as he truly believed that she was innocent, although that was not yet proven. He started investigating the moment he left Tammy. His tactic was simple: to put pressure on each of the five suspects. That way, he might get somewhere, he thought.

The first person to be interviewed was Bess Salting. She said that she was in the restroom, talking to Tracy, and that was all that she had said, until now.

"What do you want?" said Bess.

"I am investigating the murder of Barry Scott," said Coarse.

"Not another one!" cried Bess. "I'm sick of police officers! Can't you just let the dead rest in peace, and I don't mean Barry Scott!"

"It's not as simple as that," Coarse explained. "You see, Tammy Williams has been arrested for the brutal murder of Barry Scott."

"So it was her?" asked Bess.

"Possible, but Tammy maintains her innocence and has asked me to investigate Scott's death."

"You're wasting your time. It probably was her."

"If you look at it mathematically, Miss, you will see that it was probably not her. There were six established suspects. Therefore, the chances that Tammy Williams is the killer is one in six."

"Well, one in five to me, because I know that I did not do it, and I knew that Tracy did not do it, so it's a one in four chance to me."

"You say that Tracy did not do it because she was with you, but what about her alibi?"

"I don't follow."

"Who gives you an alibi? Tracy. Who gives Tracy an alibi? You. This is a traditional conspiracy technique, although it is not a very good one. Your alibi is not the most watertight of ones. You are still a suspect in my eyes."

"Alright, you've made your point, but you still can't prove it was me!" Bess replied, grinning.

Coarse knew that that was right: he could not prove it...yet. He had a very similar conversation with Tracy, and her responses were similar to Bess', as if it had been a scripted performance. However, Coarse continued to the brother of Bess, William.

William claimed that he was at a table with Linda. In order to prove, or disprove, this statement, Coarse looked at the CCTV, which was now available. Unfortunately, the results proved to be inconclusive, because as usual, on the screen, not much can be seen but a few blobs and black and white. It was like looking at an ultrasound scan with untrained eyes. No information could be retrieved, although Coarse thought that he had seen two people sitting at the table where William said he and Linda were, but he could not identify them.

"So, you claim to be here?" asked Coarse.

"I was here," William replied.

"But you might not have been," said Coarse. "You could have actually been outside. Nobody would have noticed you. You could be the killer."

"But you can't prove it," said William, smugly.

Linda had said exactly the same thing.

Joseph was the final one of the five to be interviewed. He did not say much, which made Coarse even more suspicious of him. His simple reply was, "You can't prove it."

Coarse thought that that was strange. Were they all in it together? It certainly appeared that way, and if only one person had planned it all, it seemed to him that there was a conspiracy of silence between the five of them.

Chapter 9

While Coarse tried his best to find out who the real killer of Barry Scott was (and failing), Tammy sat alone in her cell, wondering what her fate would be. She had two and a half months to wait until the trial, which seemed like it was years away. Still, she knew that she was going to get sent down anyway, unless Coarse saved her. Nobody else would listen to her, so Coarse was her only hope. She had thought about it herself, but was too tired and focused on surviving in prison, so she could not think about it in too much depth.

It was still her first official day of being in prison, and a guard opened the door to inform her that she was allowed out for one hour to exercise. This terrified her—having to face psychopaths, with barely anybody there to help if something happened. She knew that she might as well have faced it sooner or later.

Tammy left the cell, and walked over to an empty, scruffy looking table. She did not want to sit near anyone, and hoped that nobody would bother to notice

35

her, but, as luck would have it, a muscular woman, who looked as though she could beat Tammy to a pulp in seconds, approached.

"What are you in for, then?" she said, taking a seat.

"Murder," Tammy quietly replied.

"So you're a lifer then?" the woman asked in a rather friendly tone of voice.

"I'm waiting for my trial yet," Tammy said, still frightened.

"Oh, right," replied the woman. "Well, it's not as bad as you think here. They're alright; we're on the nice wing, even though it's full of murderers."

"Are they really alright?" asked Tammy.

"Well, you are, aren't you? And I am, and I killed someone!"

The woman then proceeded to ask Tammy about the circumstances of Scott's death, to which Tammy provided the same answers as before when in interrogation.

"She was a police officer," a voice in the background said, referring to Tammy.

Tammy froze for a second. She had no idea who said that. Then, she looked across the room, and the penny dropped: Libby was in the same wing as her. Libby. She was the psychotic serial killer who Tammy had arrested a couple of months before.

"She was the one who got me arrested for the murders!" screamed Libby, pointing at Tammy. "If it wasn't for her, then I wouldn't be here!"

"You what!" screamed the seemingly nice woman who had conversed with Tammy.

"I don't know what she's talking about," cried Tammy, in desperation. "She's crazy!"

"I'm not!" cried Libby, "I told you, Laura, about the one who had me arrested. Her name was Tammy Williams, who was a young woman!"

"She did," replied Laura.

Several large woman circled Tammy. There was no hope for her. One of them jumped on her, and the rest followed and then everything went blank, but Tammy remembered being pulled out of the pile of women by one of the guards. She was then escorted to another quiet room, and she was left there.

Later that day, at dinner time, Tammy was allowed out again, but forced to eat separately from the others, given the circumstances. She could still see the women who had attacked her through the bars, though, including Libby. Libby made a surprising move: she approached Tammy.

"How've you been?" asked Libby.

"How do you think?" Tammy replied, "and why do you even want to talk to me?"

"Because I have nobody else to talk to. Deep down, I really admire you for what you did. I am now starting to realize that what I did was wrong. I've had time to think about it. I was...still am crazy. I appreciate the fact that you want to do good for the community."

"Well," Tammy begun, lost for words, "what you have to say does not interest me right now, because I have other priorities."

"I was a vet, you know," said Libby. "Can't you see, Tammy? We are similar!"

"But I didn't kill anyone!" Tammy protested.

"That's what they all say," said Libby. "You did, really."

"Are you wearing a wire?" asked a suspicious Tammy.

"No," replied Libby, "and I'm not trying to get you to confess. The point is, we need each other in this place. Now that the truth about you has come out, you have no way of going back. You are going to be tortured. You will suffer for the rest of your life. It's happening to me now. I don't want to come out of my cell because a big gang of them usually bully me. I hate my life so much and I would do anything to kill myself, but they have me on suicide watch. I can't cope in here, and the same thing will happen to you. So, why don't we just talk to each other about our problems, and we might get somewhere—who knows?"

What Libby said frightened Tammy. Was this the end for her? Was she going to suffer non-stop?

"You got what you deserved," Tammy argued, "and you might then truly realize that what you did was wrong!"

Tammy got up and returned to her cell, more determined than ever to get out of the place.

Chapter 10

Coarse paid a visit to Tammy the following day to tell her what he had learned. In the visiting room, a few of the women glared at her. She tried to ignore it, but it was no use.

"It's early days, yet, Tammy," he said to her, trying to comfort her.

Tammy felt let down.

"But I want to get out of here now!" she cried helpless and impatient.

"I will get to the bottom of this," he said, determined to solve the murder before the end, "but there is one thing that you can do to help me: can you go through the entire night with me, remembering every single last detail?"

Tammy explained all that she could remember about that night. Every detail was mentioned, including what had happened after the murder. It had gone through her mind several times before assisting her in retelling events.

After that, it was time to go. Coarse left the building, thinking through what Tammy had said. Just then, an idea came into his head. Was this the moment of truth? Had he figured out the killer? It was doubtful, but perhaps one thing, one tiny thing, could solve the case.

First, he needed to visit the police station. He talked with a few police officers downstairs about a specific thing that they had witnessed on the night of the murder; it was minor, but important. Coarse then had a quick discussion with the rest of the team. He talked to Miranda first.

"Do you really think she did it?" asked Coarse.

"I think it's certainly possible," replied Miranda, grinning. "Anyway, I don't like Tammy that much, , so I hope she gets sent down for life if she's found guilty."

"And what about you, Pam?" he asked.

"I don't know," Pam replied. "I don't know what to think."

"Later," said Coarse, "I would like to ask you all to gather round, while I explain something to you. I just want to hear your thoughts."

"Why not now?" asked Pam.

"Later," Coarse replied, firmly.

He rushed out, thanking the police officers who had helped him identify something.

His final journey was to a woman's house. Coarse knew this woman from before, and he asked her if he could go into her bathroom, explaining everything, and found what he was looking for: he had solved the murder.

Chapter 11

Coarse rushed back to the police station to deliver the important news, carrying the evidence with him. He now knew without a doubt who the killer was, and he had evidence of that. He was ready to explain how and why the murderer did what they did.

"Ladies and gentlemen," begun Coarse.

Miranda was quick to interrupt. "Here we go, another one of Tammy's master revelations!" she said, jokingly.

"Please, hush!" Coarse silenced her. "I am here to announce who the real killer of Barry Scott is. I missed it, and surprisingly, so did Tammy. I bet the thought had not crossed her mind, for once. Anyway, I am not going to make things tense. The murderer is in this very room. Isn't that right, Miranda?"

Everyone looked at Miranda.

"You must be mad!" she cried.

"No, I am not mad. In fact, you are the one who is mad, isn't that right?"

"Hang on a minute!" cried the boss.

"Allow me to explain everything," said Coarse. "Let's think back to the night of the murder, shall we? On the night of the murder, Miranda had asked Angela what perfume she was wearing. Angela replied with the name of it. I have Angela's signature to prove that. Anyway, now that Miranda had Angela's perfume, all that she needed to do was mix Tammy's with it. Miranda knew what perfume Tammy used because she had previously asked her that as well.

"While Angela flirted with Barry, Miranda mixed Angela's perfume with Tammy's and placed some of the mixture on herself. When Angela approached Barry Scott and kissed him, her scent would get on him, yes? But then when he was murdered, the police would identify a certain smell. This was exactly the same smell as in Tammy's perfume bottle, which had been mixed with Angela's. This gave the police the impression that Tammy had been in close contact to Barry."

"I am so confused!" said Mitchell.

"Take one moment to think over what I had said, and it will become clear to you. Next, one of the murder weapons, a metal crowbar, was found in Tammy's car. Confusion was created because she had left her keys on a table for five minutes when she went to the restroom. However, nobody had left the table, although they had all seen the keys. Actually, Miranda had stolen Tammy's keys after the murder, when everybody was distracted. Therefore, Miranda was able to make it look impossible that nobody else could take the keys from Tammy, but Tammy."

"You're crazy!" Miranda protested.

Coarse continued. "Miranda said she saw a murder weapon in Tammy's front garden, in a bush. Miranda put gloves on. Actually, she had the sharp knife concealed in her sleeve, so when it came to picking it out of the bush, there were no fingerprints of hers on the knife. Nobody had gone to Tammy's house in between the murder and the discovery of the knife, so no one else could have possibly put the knife there, other than the murderer. It is easy to see that this murderer was Miranda."

The others looked around at Miranda, who was shaking.

"You hated Tammy, didn't you?" asked Coarse.

Miranda nodded, before breaking down.

"I can't believe this!" screamed Pam.

"But you believed that Tammy was capable of murder. When Tammy is released later today, you owe her one big apology."

Pam nodded, before taking Miranda into questioning.

An hour later, Tammy returned to the police station a free woman. She wanted to see Miranda being taken away for good.

Miranda left the station in handcuffs.

"You bitch!" she cried to Tammy, before being escorted into the police van. "You won't get away with this! You will live to regret this, Tammy Williams!"

Tammy still had one more person to thank: Coarse.

"I still can't believe she had not crossed my mind," said Tammy. "It was screaming at me in the face the whole time."

"Well, it's all over now," said Coarse. "Are you going back to work here?"

"No," Tammy replied. "I can't work here after what happened. I can find somewhere else, somewhere."

Before they parted, they took a second to look at each other, and did something completely shocking: they kissed.

But Tammy stopped. "Goodbye, George," she said, "and I'll make sure the papers remember you for what you did for me."

That was Tammy's last words to Coarse, before she departed into the sunset, not knowing what her next adventure would be.

About the Author

Brie Krauss lives in the United States with her family. Though not planning on becoming a writer, she had a few murder mysteries rolling around in her head and decided to write them on day, mostly so she could stop thinking about them. Always a fan of novellas, and quick entertainment, she kept the Closed Case stories short on purpose and hopes you enjoy them.

More by Brie Kraus

Closed case

Curious Confession
Murder on the Eiffel Tower
Over The Hills

Other Books

Don't Ask
I Hate You Rock Stars

www.ingramcontent.com/pod-product-compliance
Lightning Source LLC
Chambersburg PA
CBHW050835180626
46814CB00004B/1631